AN AMISH YEAR

To Marcia
—R. A.
This book is dedicated with love to Bryant
—P. P.

With thanks to Fannie, Rachel, Lydia, Sam, Amos, Sara, Lizzie, and Jeannie.
The illustrator would like to thank the Clemmens family for modeling throughout this book, with special thanks to Lara as the main character.

Atheneum Books for Young Readers
An imprint of Simon & Schuster Children's Publishing Division
1230 Avenue of the Americas
New York, New York 10020

Book design by Nina Barnett

The text of this book is set in Weiss.
The illustrations are rendered in pastels.

Printed in Hong Kong

2   4   6   8   10   9   7   5   3   1

Library of Congress Cataloging-in-Publication Data
Ammon, Richard.
An Amish year / by Richard Ammon; illustrated by Pamela Patrick.—1st ed.
p.   cm.
Summary: An Amish girl describes a year in her life and the activities that fill it, from early spring
through the following winter.
ISBN 0-689-82622-2
1. Amish—United States—Social life and customs—Juvenile literature. 2. Children—United States—
Social life and customs—Juvenile literature. [1. Amish—Social life and customs. 2. Pennsylvania Dutch—
Social life and customs.] I. Patrick, Pamela, ill. II. Title.
E184.M45A455   2000   973'.0287—dc21   98-52806

FIRST
EDITION

AN AMISH YEAR

by RICHARD AMMON
illustrated by PAMELA PATRICK

ATHENEUM BOOKS FOR YOUNG READERS

I know when spring is coming long before buds begin to blossom. Brightly colored kites sail high above silos and leafless trees.

I can't wait to fly our kite, but first I must help with chores. Early every morning and every evening, I help with the milking. I know the names of every one of our forty-four brown-and-white holstein cows.

After milking, I help my brother Danny feed our horses—Roy, a saddlebred who pulls our *Doch Waggle* (buggy), and our three pairs of Belgian draft horses, who work in the fields.

My favorite chore is tending the chickens. In the quiet of the evening my older sister Fannie and I sing as we feed the chickens and carefully gather eggs.

After chores, I fly my kite, which looks like a great red-and-yellow bird with a long tail. The reel spins as I let it climb the sky until there is no string wrapped around the spool. I wonder what it sees, perched near the clouds.

Early Easter morning, I help my younger sister, Rachel, hunt for eggs that I hid last evening.

Then we drive Roy to Uncle Amos's place for church. We hold church in our homes every other Sunday. On the Sundays in between, we spend a quiet morning reading. Afternoons are for visiting family and friends.

Church lasts about three hours. The minister preaches in German, and we slowly sing hymns, also in German. Mothers keep the little children busy with small dolls they make by curling their handkerchiefs.

After church we eat a light meal of Lebanon bologna, cheese, pickles, homemade bread, and snitz pies made from dried apples. Later, the men go outside to talk about the sermon and news of people from other valleys. Inside, the women fuss over the babies while we children race outdoors to play.

Easter Monday is a day for visiting. It's a good day to take a walk. I look for crocuses and robins, early signs of spring. The boys go fishing at Uncle Steve's pond.

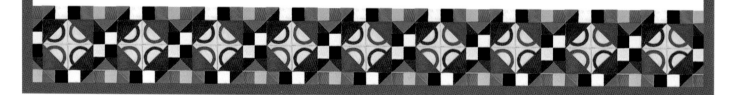

In the early spring, it's time to get Mamm's garden ready for planting. After Danny plows, I rake out the soil as Mamm plants radishes, spring onions, lettuce, and peas. Datt can't wait to eat onion-and-radish sandwiches!

In April, I help Mamm put in broccoli and cabbage plants. We sow seeds of sweet corn, beets, and spinach in long, straight rows. In deeper rows, we drop seed potatoes.

After the last frost, we put in tomato and pepper plants, celery, and rows and rows of beans. I push cantaloupe, cucumber, zucchini, and pumpkin seeds into separate mounds of brown earth. Then we edge the garden with a variety of flowers.

Another sure sign of the season is spring cleaning. Quilts hang from long wash lines stretching from the house to the corner of the barn. On my hands and knees, I wash the floors with a rag and a bucket of sudsy water.

In May, I look forward to our school picnic. Around eleven o'clock, we scholars see buggies pulling up to the rail at the far end of the school yard. Our mothers are bringing food, lots of food—hot dogs and hamburgers, potato salad and potato chips, red beet eggs, celery and carrots, plenty of drinks, and shoofly pie. Even some fathers come. I think they don't want to miss out on all that good food.

After we eat, it's time for softball. It's boys against girls! Sara, our teacher, is the pitcher for both sides, and Datt is the catcher. When it's my turn to bat, I smack the ball hard. It flies high and deep right into Sam Esh's cow pasture.

We play until Mamm calls from the buggy, *"Kum, Lizzie. Hole Rachel und Danny. Es ist Tziet fer geh."* ("Come, Lizzie. Fetch Rachel and Danny. It's time to go.")

What I like most about summer is going barefooted, feeling the cool garden earth beneath my feet.

Mamm's garden bursts with color—pink and white petunias, orange and yellow marigolds, flaming cockscomb, and red and yellow gladiolus standing in tall, straight lines. Between rows of corn, I hoe stubborn weeds.

In the evening, after helping with chores—milking the cows and feeding the chickens—I mow the yard. Grass clippings spray out onto my toes as I push the mower in neat rows. When I finish, the lawn looks so smooth, like it's covered with a green blanket.

One evening, we hear the siren wail and see smoke rising over the hill. Our English neighbor races his pickup truck down our lane.

"It's Steve's place," he calls. We crawl in and hurry down the valley road. The fire trucks are already pumping water from the pond onto the roof.

That night, Steve's family stays with us. The next morning, Datt and my brothers, uncles, and cousins begin repairing Steve and Rachel's charred home.

While supplies are delivered, Danny and I help clean up the mess of burned things in the basement. I'm surprised that Rachel's jars of strawberry jam made it through the fire.

After the men set new joists in place, hammers thunder as they nail down new floorboards and siding. By week's end, the outside looks as if nothing happened.

Summer is the time for making hay. When the sky is clear, Datt mows the field of alfalfa. After it dries for a day in the hot sun, Danny rakes it into rows.

The next day, I help Datt and Danny hitch up the pairs of Belgian horses. Although they weigh almost a ton, they're gentle and willing workers. I stand on the cart with Danny as he drives the baler. The baler scoops up the dry alfalfa and presses it into shape. As the bale is pushed out, the baler ties it with twine.

Datt stacks the bales on the wagon until it is piled high. Then we unhook the wagon load of bales and latch on an empty wagon. Datt hauls the hay wagon to the barn, where he and my older brother Jake stack the bales in the loft.

Around four o'clock, we stop to milk the cows and eat a sandwich. Then it's back to the field to bring in the last wagon loads of hay.

In the cool evening, we gather around the picnic table under the maple tree, where Mamm and I dish out bowls of ice cream.

Friday is my birthday! At supper, Mamm and Datt give me my birthday present, a scooter. I try it out, speeding up and down our lane.

After evening chores, I see Uncle Steve driving his buggy toward our place. Uncle Amos's and Uncle Levi's horses trot behind. My uncles, aunts, and cousins have come to surprise me!

My cousins and I get up a game of volleyball. The lead goes back and forth. With the game tied as the sun sets, the boys pull the buggies around in a big circle and turn on the buggy lights. Now we can finish our game.

Then it's inside for cake and ice cream.

Afterwards we sing "Gott ist die Liebe" and other songs. Fannie takes out her harmonica and plays along. I cannot imagine a more wonderful birthday.

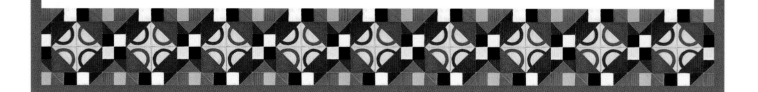

This fall, I begin fourth grade. As Rachel, Danny, and I walk down the lane between cornfields to our one-room school, we see the farmers in the fields harvesting corn.

Inside our schoolhouse, we scholars—grades one through eight—study our lessons. Our day begins when Sara rings the bell. Like all Amish, she went to school only through the eighth grade. After taking attendance, she reads verses from the Bible, but we do not say the Pledge of Allegiance. There is no flag in our school.

I really like when Sara calls out arithmetic problems. "Twenty-seven divided by three, plus three, times three, divided by four." I have to be on my toes to be the first one to shout out the correct answer.

History and geography are my favorite subjects. I like reading about people from long ago and places that are far away.

We are never given homework because all Amish children have chores to do around the home or farm.

We speak Pennsylvanish Deitsch (Pennsylvania Dutch) around home. So, first graders come to school speaking this language. But because our lessons and books are in English, by Christmas most first graders can read their English primers.

Long ago, Amish traveled from Switzerland to an area along the Rhine River between Germany and France, where people speak German. When the Amish came to the United States, English folks in Pennsylvania mistakenly thought the German word for "German," *Deutsch*, sounded like "Dutch." Ever since, our language has been known as Pennsylvania Dutch.

If I wanted to say, "Good morning. How are you?" I would say, *"Gut marriye. Wie bischt du?"*

The canning season began with cherries. In early summer, I picked cherries, dropping them into a stainless steel pail. Sitting on the back porch, I used a hairpin to scoop out the cherry pits. Canned cherries will make wonderful pies this winter.

In autumn, Mamm and I make chow chow. I help Mamm cook each of the vegetables—five different kinds of beans, as well as cauliflower, carrots, corn, white onions, and cabbage—separately until each is tender but crisp. Then we heat the vegetables together in a vinegar syrup before spooning the chow chow into jars.

Because I have small hands, I get the job of slipping peaches and pears into glass jars, too.

With the last lid sealed, I help carry the jars to the basement. One slips from my hands—*CRASH!* While helping me clean up the mess, Mamm says, "That's all right. This happens once every year."

When all's done, the cold cellar looks beautiful, lined from floor to ceiling with shelves upon shelves of colorful jars of fruits and vegetables for our winter meals.

Weddings are held on Tuesdays and Thursdays in November. When Anna and Samuel were married last November, almost three hundred people crowded into our home. Except for brothers and sisters of the bride or groom, children do not attend weddings because they are in school. The wedding ceremony is part of the church service and lasts almost three hours.

Afterwards it's time for dinner—roast chicken and cooked celery. All day, tables are piled with cakes and cookies. When Samuel and Anna sat in the *Eck,* the special corner for the bride and groom, I sneaked up to the window and tapped on it. Anna opened it a crack and slipped me some candy.

In the afternoon, I tiptoed upstairs and placed a broom across the doorway. When Anna came out, she stepped across the broom, going from maiden to homemaker.

If Mamm and Datt don't have a wedding to go to on Thanksgiving Day, all my aunts and uncles and cousins will gather for a big Thanksgiving dinner. If someone raised a turkey, we'll roast it. If not, chicken tastes fine.

Christmas is an important holiday for us. Santa Claus doesn't come, and we have no Christmas tree or other decorations in our homes. But in the spirit of the Wise Men, we exchange gifts. This past Christmas, Mamm and Datt gave me a black handbag just like Mamm's.

On the last school day before Christmas, we scholars put on a Christmas program after lunch. Our family buggies pull up to the school. Sitting on benches in the back of the room, parents, grandparents, and older sisters listen to us sing Christmas carols and watch our skits.

Just like the English, we have plenty to eat at Christmas. I help Mamm bake cookies and dip pretzels in chocolate. My favorite treats are chocolate-coated peanut butter balls.

The Second Day of Christmas is a time for visiting. This year, all our aunts and uncles and cousins visit Grossdawdy and Grossmammy. They live in the Grossdawdy house attached to Uncle Amos's.

Altogether, there must be fifty people for dinner. We have roast chicken, potatoes, and vegetables, topped off with pumpkin pie.

The snow's deep, so we're soon sledding down the hill through the orchard. One trail is steep and fast with lots of bumps. Another trail is not as scary.

The next day it's back to school. We go to school between Christmas and New Year's Day so that we can get out early in the spring to help around the farm.

In the winter we also like to skate. After evening chores, we build a big bonfire and skate on Uncle Steve's pond. The boys play hockey near the light of the fire, while we girls skate crack-the-whip at the far end.

Sometimes on cold winter evenings, we play board games. I especially like Monopoly.

Other evenings, I sit by the stove and read. I've read all the *Little House* books, so tonight I am beginning *Misty of Chincoteague.*

In February, we make and send valentine cards. There's a big box in school where scholars drop their valentines. Near the end of the school day, the teacher picks two people to deliver the mail.

Longer days tell us it will soon be spring again. Each year brings new wonders and joyful times for me, my family, and our friends.

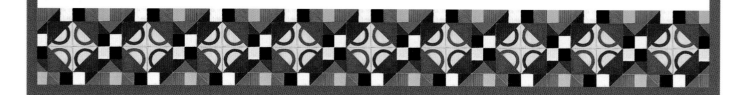

Author's Note

In 1693 in Switzerland, Jakob Ammann founded the Amish faith. The first known group of Amish landed in Philadelphia in 1737 to escape religious persecution they faced in Europe. Because the Amish didn't want to look like those army officers with mustaches and brass buttons who tormented them, married Amish men grow beards but no mustaches, and they fasten their coats with hooks and eyes, not buttons. Even the women attach their capes and aprons to their dresses with plain straight pins.

They dress alike because they believe that no one is more important than anyone else. It wouldn't be right if someone felt proud because that person had fancier sneakers than the rest, or if someone had a prettier dress or a more expensive shirt. Because they feel everyone is equal, they also address each other by first names, even teachers and bishops.

The community is the most important part of Amish life. It includes parents, grandparents, brothers and sisters, aunts and uncles, the families who go to their church, and other Amish relatives and friends. They take care of each other, which is why no Amish person is ever in need. There are no home-less Amish.

The Amish live simply, but it's not true that they don't like new things. They use pocket calculators to figure out how much to charge at their fruit and vegetable stands. Every morn-ing and evening, farmers start up diesel engines to run the milking machines, and Amish women cook and bake with gas stoves and keep food fresh in gas refrigerators.

Amish just don't believe that all new gadgets are good for them. That's why they have no elec-tric lines running to their homes. That means no television, because they believe that many television programs are not worthwhile. While they may talk on the telephone, they do not have phones in their homes. Some Amish need to use the telephone to order supplies for their shops. And they call 911 to report an emergency. But they don't feel they should spend time on the phone gossiping. They would rather visit each other in person.

Old Order Amish do not own or drive cars, although they are allowed to ride in cars. Church leaders feel their people should not stray too far from their families. Besides, it would not be right for someone to feel proud because he owned a fancy car.

Traveling by horse and buggy does take longer. A trip that would take a half hour by car takes the Amish about two hours. But going slowly allows them to see so many things English people miss as they speed past.

Being Amish often means giving up many modern conveniences. But sometimes the old ways provide special joys. Most of all, tradition allows the Amish to maintain their faith and culture.

—R.A.